BIRDS of a FEATHER

Tweety and SYLVESTER in

By Jean Lewis
Illustrated by Joe Messerli

A GOLDEN BOOK • NEW YORK

Western Publishing Company, Inc., Racine, Wisconsin 53404

Library of Congress Catalog Card Number: 91-75923 ISBN: 0-307-00129-6 MCMXCII

"I'm so excited about going to the bird show!" said Granny, putting on her best hat.

"We mustn't be late," said her friend Gladys. "There will be so many lovely birds to see.

"Tweety is pretty, too," Gladys added. "I must take a picture of him before we leave."

"Tweety's also clever," said Granny. She quickly found
a videotape she wanted to play. "Watch this! Now, Tweety,"
she prompted, "sing along with Luigi."

Tweety made Granny proud as he sang along with
the famous opera singer Luigi Canelone.

"That's amazing!" said Gladys. "Luigi Canelone is going to judge the Talent Contest. You must enter Tweety in the show. I just happen to have an entry form."

Suddenly Gladys sniffed the air. "Is something burning?" she asked.

"It's only Sylvester," said Granny. "He's always jealous of Tweety.

"Tweety, dear, how would you like to sing at the bird show?" asked Granny, taking him out of his cage.

"Oooh, yes, Granny!" said Tweety.

"Then you shall," said Granny.

"Sufferin' succotash!" Sylvester exclaimed to himself. "That dumb bird isn't the only performer in this house!"

Sylvester leapt into the air, hoping to rise gracefully over the floor lamp.

He and the lamp crashed to the floor, much to Granny's dismay.

"Try not to wreck the house while we're gone," Granny told Sylvester. Then she slammed the front door behind her.

Sylvester discovered a bird show entry form on the floor. "There will be *hundreds* of birds," it said. "Canaries, cockatoos, parakeets, parrots . . ." Sylvester's mouth began to water. Tweety was only one small bird, hardly a mouthful. But the bird show would be a feast! Sylvester had to find a way to get to the show.

"I'll disguise myself as a bird!" Sylvester exclaimed, racing up to the attic.

In the attic the frantic cat found a large bird cage.
"It's just my size!" he said. Then he ran to a dusty trunk
and began pulling out old clothes and scattering
mothballs.

"Ah-CHOO!" Sylvester sneezed. "Nothing but dust
in here," he groaned. "Wait—what's this?

"Sufferin' succotash—feathers!" cried Sylvester. "Just what I need!"

He had wrapped himself in an ancient orange-and-green feather boa. "It's a cat! It's a bird! No, it's a catbird!" Sylvester cried, flapping his wings.

Sylvester quickly made a sign for his cage that said:
FAR EASTERN CATBIRD.

Then he grabbed the cage and raced downstairs. Soon
he was on his way to the show, trailing the feather boa
behind him.

Sylvester headed for town. As he neared the show tent, he followed the sounds of "Polly want a cracker!" and a growing chorus of birdcalls.

Then the sly cat crawled under the tent and found a quiet corner beside a pile of birdseed bags. After draping himself in the feather boa, he hopped into his cage and shut the door.

WELCOME TO THE BIRD SHOW

Before Sylvester could plan his feast, he spotted Granny and Gladys heading toward him.

"Time to disappear!" he cried, pushing the door of the cage. The door wouldn't open.

"It's locked!" wailed Sylvester. "And I haven't got a key!"

Sylvester stuck his legs through the bars and tried to walk away, cage and all.

When that didn't work, he buried himself in his borrowed feathers, pretending to be asleep. "Maybe they won't notice me," he muttered.

Granny stopped when she saw the cage. "That looks like the old cage in my attic," she said.

" 'Far Eastern Catbird,' " said Gladys, reading Sylvester's sign. "Must be a new species. My, what colorful plumage that bird has!"

"That's Aunt Mabel's old feather boa!" said Granny. Sylvester shuddered.

"And that's Sylvester!" cried Granny.

FAR EASTERN CATBIRD

"Sylvester, don't you dare move until I get back," said Granny sternly. "We have to take Tweety to the talent contest now. Luigi Canelone will be waiting!"

From his cage, Sylvester was forced to hear Tweety sing along with Luigi.

Luigi's voice was loud, but Tweety's was high—a perfect four octaves higher than Luigi's. The crowd cheered and applauded.

Before the awards were even given out, Mr. Botts of Botts' Best Birdseed offered Tweety a contract. "He will be great for my TV birdseed commercial," Mr. Botts told Granny.

But Granny refused politely. "Thank you, Mr. Botts," she said. "But I want Tweety to have a normal homelife."

Granny's conversation was interrupted. It was time for Luigi Canelone to award the prize for Most Talented Bird in the show.

Tweety sang all the way home from the show.
Sylvester sat in the backseat, surrounded by bags of
Botts' Best Birdseed—part of Tweety's prize.
With the feather boa wrapped around his head,
Sylvester was able to drown out Tweety's annoying
chirping. Luckily, he couldn't hear Granny either when
she said, "I do hope I can remember where I put the key
to that old cage. Now, let me think . . ."

"And the winner is . . . Tweety!" said Luigi, attaching
a big blue ribbon to Tweety's cage. Tweety sang happily.
There were cheers and applause from everybody—
except Sylvester.